THIS LITTLE TIGER BOOK BELONGS TO:

_____

_____

_____

_____

DISCARDE

D0363302

*To Ben, who painted Tucker pink*
*when **he** was a little monkey*
– S S

*To Mary*
– N S

LITTLE TIGER PRESS
An imprint of Magi Publications
1 The Coda Centre, 189 Munster Road,
London SW6 6AW
www.littletigerpress.com

First published in Great Britain 2007
This edition published 2012
Text copyright © Steve Smallman 2007
Illustrations copyright © Nick Schon 2007
Steve Smallman and Nick Schon have asserted
their rights to be identified as the author and
illustrator of this work under the Copyright,
Designs and Patents Act, 1988

ISBN 978-1-84895-282-9

Printed in China • LTP/1800/0294/1211

10 9 8 7 6 5 4 3 2 1

# THE MONKEY WITH A BRIGHT BLUE BOTTOM

Steve Smallman

Nick Schon

LITTLE TIGER PRESS
London

A long time ago, when the world was quite new,
A monkey sat watching the birds as they flew.
Like feathery rainbows they flashed through the air.
"How come they're so pretty," he thought. "It's not fair!"

All round him were creatures of every sort,
Some fat and some skinny, some tall and some short,
But none of them purple or yellow or blue;
They all looked as dull as an elephant poo.

The monkey walked down to the stream with a sigh,
Then a vivid blue kingfisher bird darted by.
He followed it down to a gap in the rushes
And there was a paintbox with one or two brushes.

He snatched up the paintbox as quick as a wink,
Tried painting some flowers and then had a think:
"Somebody painted this kingfisher blue,
I'm going to paint all the animals too!"

The animals always get out of the sun
And go for a nap at a quarter to one.
So when he was sure everybody was sleeping,
With paintbox and brushes the monkey came creeping.

He painted some frogs and a couple of snakes
And thought to himself, "What a difference it makes!"
Then feeling much bolder, the cheeky young fellow
Set to and painted a leopard bright yellow.

Just then the big cat gave a growl in his sleep
And monkey shot into a tree with a leap.
The black paint dropped out with a splash from the box,
And fell on the leopard in little black spots.

"That's great!" said the monkey,
    then, just for a laugh,
He painted brown squares on a yellow giraffe,
Black stripes on a zebra and white on a skunk,
And both on the lemur asleep in his bunk.

"Hee hee!" laughed the monkey, "I'm having such fun!"
Then he spotted a bear fast asleep in the sun.
He took out his brush and then, what a surprise,
He painted white spectacles round the bear's eyes!

Bear woke with a start and yelled,
    "WHAT DID YOU DO?"
Which woke up the rest of the animals too.
The monkey was so scared he practically fainted,
Surrounded by all of the creatures he'd painted.

They all started yelling till bear shouted, "HUSH!"
Then quietly picked up the paintbox and brush.
He painted the monkey's face red, white and blue.
And then for good luck did his bottom end too!

And still to this day when the monkey goes by,
The animals giggle, they laugh till they cry.
His bum is still blue as a bright summer sky,
He looks like a clown – and now you know why!

# BRIGHTEN YOUR DAY WITH THESE BOOKS FROM LITTLE TIGER PRESS

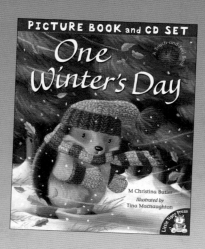

PICTURE BOOK and CD SET

One Winter's Day

A touch-and-feel book

M Christina Butler
Illustrated by
Tina Macnaughton

PICTURE BOOK and CD SET

The Very Greedy Bee

Steve Smallman    Jack Tickle

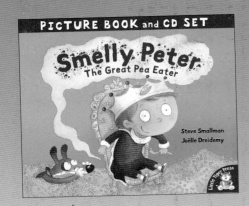

PICTURE BOOK and CD SET

Smelly Peter
The Great Pea Eater

Steve Smallman
Joëlle Dreidemy

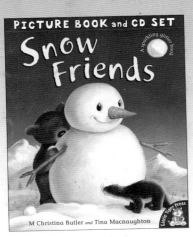

PICTURE BOOK and CD SET

Snow Friends

A sparkling glitter book

M Christina Butler and Tina Macnaughton

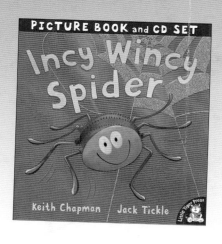

PICTURE BOOK and CD SET

Incy Wincy Spider

Keith Chapman    Jack Tickle

For information regarding any of the above titles or for our catalogue, please contact us:
Little Tiger Press, 1 The Coda Centre, 189 Munster Road, London SW6 6AW
Tel: 020 7385 6333 • Fax: 020 7385 7333 • E-mail: info@littletiger.co.uk • www.littletigerpress.com